MW01473881

weebee Series 2

by R M Price-Mohr

# The troll

weebee book 15

Published by Crossbridge Books
Worcester

ISBN 978-1-913946-34-0

British Library Cataloguing Publication Data

A catalogue record for this book is available
from the British Library

# The weebees

Grog      Pip      Tod      Mop

Jig      Zon      Flup      Saff

One day Grog, Pip, Tod and Zon went for a long walk.

They walked to the woods and then to the old wall.

Next they walked across the yellow field.

When they got to the little bridge they sat down to rest.

"Where do we go now?" asked Zon.

"I want to cross the bridge," said Grog.

Grog, Pip, Tod and Zon did not see the troll under the bridge.

They did not hear him.

The troll was very cross.

"I want to go over the bridge too," said Tod.

They all went to the bridge.

Up jumped the troll.

He was very cross.

He looked very scary.

"You can not come across my bridge," said the troll.

"It is a scary monster," said Zon.

"Did you hear what he said?" asked Pip.

"I am not scared," said Grog.

"What will you do to me?" asked Grog.

"I will put you in the water," said the troll.

Pip, Tod and Zon were scared of the troll.

Grog was not scared.

"I will cross over the bridge," said Grog.

Zon was scared.

He did not want to look.

The troll was very small.

He was not scary but he looked very cross.

"Where do you want to go?" asked the troll.

"Just into the next field to have a rest before we go home," said Grog.

The troll went into the field with Grog.

Pip, Tod and Zon walked over the bridge.

26

They all sat in the field for a rest.

The troll told Grog that he did not have a home.

Grog asked the troll to go home with him.

The troll was very happy.

They all walked back home.

CPSIA information can be obtained
at www.ICGtesting.com
Printed in the USA
LVHW021635281220
675138LV00030B/835